Stars

Stars

By Lucy Haché
Illustrations by Michael Joyal

Winnipeg

Stars

Stars copyright © 2018 Lucy Haché
Illustrations copyright © 2018 Michael Joyal

Design by M. C. Joudrey and Matthew Stevens.
Layout by Alana Brooker and Matthew Stevens.

At Bay Press logo copyright © 2018 At Bay Press

Published by At Bay Press March 2018.

All rights reserved. The use of any part of this publication, reproduced, transmitted in any form or by any means electronic, mechanical, photocopying, recording or otherwise, or stored in a retrieval system without prior written consent of the publisher or in the case of photocopying or other reprographic copying, license from the Canadian Copyright Licensing Agency-is an infringement of the copyright law.

No portion of this work may be reproduced without express written permission from At Bay Press.

ISBN 978-1-988168-10-4

Library and Archives Canada cataloguing in publication is available upon request.

Typeset in Dante
Printed and bound in Canada.

This book is printed on acid free paper that is 100% recycled ancient forest friendly (100% post-consumer recycled).

First Edition

atbaypress.com

10 9 8 7 6 5 4 3 2 1

For my mother, grandmothers and all the strong Indigenous women who have been a light in the darkness.

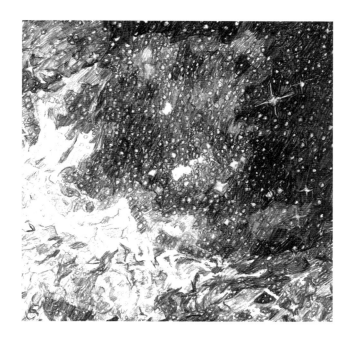

The moonless night sky stretches out above me.

Nine thousand and ninety-six flecks of light
punctuate the darkness.

I am stargazing so that I may learn a thing or two
from these ancient ones.

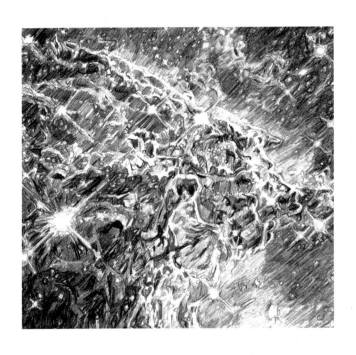

Each star is a witness to all stories, and I have forgotten how to tell my own.

My body has become heavy in the city.
It's taken on the weight of the cement, the glass,
the metal.

The persistent drone of constant frantic
movement has hypnotized me into forgetting
that I am alive.

I've carried my heavy body to where the forest meets the sea on the western edge of Vancouver Island — a place named for a man who did not belong here.

The forest and the ocean never forget that no man may claim them. As for the stars above, humans have named them too.

I am surrounded by darkness. My eyes have forgotten how to see in the night without the glow of the city lights.

I've found my way to the beach through the forest trail by looking up at the line of stars between the treetops.

The city has made me hollow, empty.
Blocking out the stars with its artificial lights and concrete buildings.

How can I learn to thrive when what gives me life is obscured and out of reach?

I have come here to see the stars better,
so that I might remember how to flourish.

As a young girl, on the clear warm nights of
summer my sister and I would camp out on the
balcony and watch shooting stars.

Each streak across the night sky lit up our minds
with a thousand possibilities as we made wish,
upon wish,
upon wish.

I don't remember what I wished for,
but I remember feeling hope.

Now, as I lay with my back upon the sand and listen to the pulse of the ocean waves, I am losing myself in the same night sky.

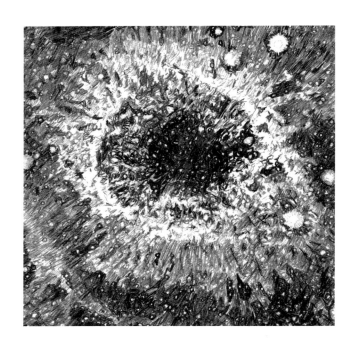

But instead of feeling the vibrancy of hope,
I feel weak and empty.

There are no shooting stars tonight.

I wish I had my mother's strength.
She fought for our rights in the '70s and the
'80s so that I may now proudly call myself a
Kwakwaka'wakw Woman, instead of
hiding behind my green eyes.

I moved off the reserve and into the city to learn how to fight like her. I went to university to sharpen my mind like hers.

But the academic institution sharpened my corners to make me fit better into a box within which I do not belong.

I tried to fight for change there too, but it only made my edges sharper.

I now know that my mother's strength came from the land, the sea, and the night sky.

The soundtrack of my childhood propelled me into the city and the academic institution, my green eyes blazing with activist passion. Buffy Sainte-Marie: "Star Walker, he's a friend of mine..." and Joni Mitchell: "We are stardust..."

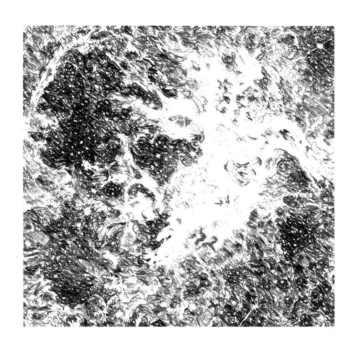

We are stardust.
When the universe was young, the first atoms that came into being were hydrogen. They combined under gravity, and the pressure and temperature became so high that the hydrogen atoms fused to form helium and then heavier elements through nuclear fusion.

Eventually, after billions of years, the star burned up and died in an immense explosion: supernova. In that moment, the star became as bright as its entire galaxy. The elements within the star were thrown out into the universe to form new planets. Our planet comes from the ashes of a dead star. Cataclysmic creation. This is one version of our creation story.

We are stardust.
But we are forced to forget.

Perhaps if we remembered then my people
wouldn't have been forcefully relocated from
their homes in 1964. Their houses burnt down,
their children's bodies and spirits bruised and
beaten in residential schools. We wouldn't carry
intergenerational trauma like a heavy
cloak of shame.

Perhaps the doctor who allowed my grandmother to die would have looked past her skin colour, her status card, and all his preconceived notions about *Indians*. He would have listened to her.
He would have helped her live.

She would have continued teaching our stories
and our language.

Everything Grandma taught me before she died
I now cling to for my survival.

I remember *tutu*.
Tutu, a word that filled me with hope as a child is now my lifeline as I search for the light that will keep me going.

A shiver runs through me, bringing me back to earth.

I have become cold from the ocean mist.

In all my years on this planet I have learned so many lessons, and yet I know nothing.

I have died and been reborn countless times.

I have learned to give more, to love more,
to burn brighter.

But burning brightly in the darkness is lonely work.

The wrong that has been done to my loved ones,
to my community, to my people, to my ancestors
is the fuel that keeps me burning.

And sometimes, I fear I will go supernova.

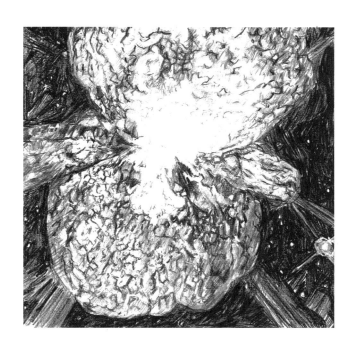

Or worse, I will turn inward and become the absence of all light — a black hole.

But then I remember who carried the light before me.

My people, and many of the peoples on the
Northwest Coast believe that *Gʷawina*
released *ƛisəla*, the largest star in our solar
system, from those who coveted it.

Shedding light on our dark world, allowing life to thrive.

Darkness created by greed. Light created by generosity.

The very meaning of my name is derived from a Latin
word for light.

This name was passed to me from my grandmother. Before that, it was a name given to my great-great-grandmother. Her mother's name was *Nakńagim*.

The light is not a burden. It's a gift.

It has been running through us for millennia,
upon millennia,
upon millennia.

When I am overflowing with emptiness yet
feel like I will burst apart, like every particle of
my being is begging to return to the night sky,
I will remember the strength of my mother,
grandmothers, great-grandmothers.

I will feel that strength wrap around me.

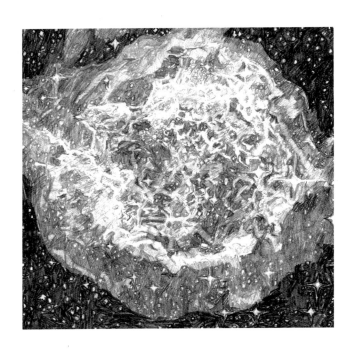

Holding all the little bits of light together.

I will continue to shine like them.

That is their gift to me, and mine to them.

I push myself up from the sand and look out
over the sea.

I can feel the northwesterly wind and the sea mist
on my skin. But I am no longer cold.

I turn back to the forest trail. This time I find my way without the help of the night sky.

I remember my way home.

Glossary: Astronomical Illustrations

Page 1 — Westerlund 2, Gum 29

Page 4 — Monkey Head Nebula - NGC 2174 and Sharpless Sh2 - 252

Page 7 — Arp 273, UGC 1810 - Interacting Galaxies

Page 11 — NGC 7640

Page 14 — Pleiades

Page 17 — Horsehead Nebula - Barnard 33

Page 20 — NGC 7293 - Helix Nebula Eye of God

Page 24 — Pillars of Creation

Page 27 — 30 Doradus - Tarantula Nebula

Page 30 — NGC 602

Page 35 — NGC 2264 - Cone Nebula

Page 40 — Supermassive black hole in the core of the elliptical galaxy Hercules A

Page 42 — NGC 6302 - Bug Nebula or Butterfly Nebula

Page 45 — NGC 7635 - Bubble Nebula

Page 47 — Homunculus Nebula, surrounding Eta Carinae

Page 50 — Sagittarius

Page 56 — Pismis 24

Page 59 — Calabash Nebula - OH 231.8+04.2

Page 62 — Cassiopeia - A

Page 65 — Orion B molecular cloud complex

Page 68 — Trumpler 14

Glossary: Kʷakʼʷala Language

kʷakʷəkəẃakʷ [kwah-kwuh-kyuh-wakw]
Kʷakʼʷala speaking people. A group of distinct First Nations tribes who live on the Central Coast of British Columbia, including north Vancouver Island and mainland British Columbia and speak different dialects of the kʷakʼʷala language.

Gwa'sala'Nakwaxda'xw [gwah-sah-lah-nak-wak-tow]
Two kʷakʷəkəẃakʷ tribes who were forcefully relocated from their traditional territories by the Canadian government in 1964. They were amalgamated and are now considered one tribe. Author Lucy Haché is a member of this tribe.

kʷakʼʷala [kwah-kwal-ah]
The language spoken by the Kʷakʷəkəẃakʷ people. Due to colonization, forced relocation from land, and residential schools, it is now considered an endangered language.

t̓ut̓u [tuu-tuu, with an explosive 't']
The stars

λ̓isəla [tlee-suh-lah, with an explosive 'tl']
The sun

Gʷaẃina [gwah-ween-ah]
Raven

Nakṅagim [nak-nah-geem]
Handling the daylight. The name of Lucy Haché's kʷakʷəkəẃakʷ great-great-great-grandmother.

About the Author

Lucy Haché, writer and adventurer of Kwakwaka'wakw/ Métis and Scottish/Irish descent. She is a member of the Gwa'sala-'Nakwaxda'xw Nations, a Kwakwaka'wakw Community on the northern tip of Vancouver Island, British Columbia. Much of her life has been spent in the forest or on the sea. When she's not surrounded by nature she writes about it. She also writes about contemporary and historical Indigenous issues.

About the Artist

Michael Joyal, Canadian watercolour artist whose work focuses on reinterpreting characters from mythology and fairy tales through a modern lens. His paintings explore roles of feminine power through feelings of strength, anger, melancholy and joy. He has exhibited in Canada and the United States. His work is held in permanent collection at the International Cryptozoology Museum and the Legislative Library of Manitoba. To view more of his art, visit leadvitamins.com